© 1998 IASOS
Published by:
Bluestar Communications Corporation
44 Bear Glenn
Woodside, CA 94062
Tel: 800-6-Bluestar

Edited by Jude Berman
Cover Art by Garret Moore, Dreaming Lizard Studios
Layout: Petra Michel

All composing, arranging, instrument-playing, recording, and mixing by Iasos

Copyright All Music: © 1998 IASOS
BMI Galaxia Creations
Photo Images Copyrighted by IASOS © 1998
Copyright Cover Illustration:
© 1998 Garret Moore & Bluestar Communications Corporation
First printing 1998

ISBN: 1-885394-30-6

All rights reserved. No part of this book or CD may be reproduced in any form without the written permission of the publishers, except for brief quotations embodied in critical articles and reviews.

Printed in China
through Palace Press International

SACRED SONIC TOOLS

#	Title	Time
1	*Pleiadian Healing Cycles*	3:28
2	*A Crystal Fountain of Light*	2:18
3	*Cloud Prayer*	5:06
4	*Fairy Dust*	2:43
5	*Woomfas (Interstellar Thunder)*	1:44
6	*Glitter Sweep (Etheric Brush)*	1:28
7	*The Transmuting Violet Flame Sound*	4:58
8	*The Bubble Massage*	4:26
9	*Fairy Laughter*	3:13
10	*Lagoon Waves*	6:59
11	*Undulating Bell Harmonics*	7:25
12	*The Angels of Purity*	5:27
13	*Brooks*	6:14
14	*The Spiral Ascensions*	2:29
15	*Silence*	1:00

Disclaimer

The effects of these sounds are primarily on your subtle-energy spiritual bodies, not your physical body. No claims, stated or implied, are made for the healing of any physical ailments. This work is not intended to replace qualified medical treatment.

Table of Contents

Introduction	7
Application Notes	15
Tips for Useful Programming of your CD Player	47
Sound as Healing Light Waves	50
Summary of the Effects	60
Functional Overview	63

Introduction to Sacred Sonic Tools

*For light-workers, therapists, hospice workers,
health care professionals, body-workers,
or anyone interested in using sound for healing, initiation,
self-improvement, or travel to other dimensions.*

Welcome to *Sacred Sonic Tools*! I hope this toolbox will provide you with an immense amount of beneficial use. To get the most out of it, please take a moment to read the next two sections:

The Basic Concept
and
Recommended Familiarization Process

The Basic Concept

The compact disc (CD) included with this book is a *toolbox* of audio tools—each with its own unique energetic effects. All of the effects are programmed to "tune-up" your energy fields in various different ways.

That is, each tool is a highly "potentized" sound, designed to powerfully influence subtle energy in a specific manner. The idea for this CD is not to play it straight through like a normal music CD, but to go directly to and play just those tracks relevant to your current application. In this way, it is like a carpenter using just the tools from his toolbox that he needs for whatever he is doing in that moment. You can use this toolbox on yourself, on another (one-on-one), or on a whole group.

Recommended Familiarization Process

Whereas for a conventional music CD you would familiarize yourself with the music by playing the CD straight through, I recommend a totally different approach for familiarizing yourself with this toolbox, so that you can quickly begin enjoying maximum benefit from it. I recommend that you select any tool whose title catches your interest. *Read* the application notes for that tool. Then *listen*—preferably with headphones—to just that one tool by selecting the appropriate track on your CD player, and then stopping the CD when that track is finished playing. After listening, I recommend you once again *read* the application notes for that tool.

Repeat this process of read/listen/read for each tool that catches your interest. You don't have to do them in order. Skip around according to your curiosity.

This process will optimize both your conceptual and your intuitive

understanding of what that tool can do for you. If you get any ideas for unique ways you can apply this particular tool in your own life, we encourage you to write down your ideas on the empty pages of the *Application Notes* for that tool or keep a notebook for those ideas.

By the way, if you come up with some novel applications for any of these tools and would like to share them with us, please contact us with your application or method of use. We love getting such feedback! Send your comments to:

Iasos
33 Varda Landing
Sausalito, CA. 94965

or email us at:
iasos@nbn.com
or
sst@bluestar.com

Understanding Your CD Player

To use this toolbox most effectively, you need to know how to directly access any set of tools you choose. This means you need to know how to program your CD player so it can play

* any sequence of tracks you choose
* in any order you choose
* and either play only once or repeatedly through a sequence of tracks until you press STOP

I highly recommend using a *programmable* CD player and studying your CD manual until this is crystal-clear. Then you can really have fun accessing what this toolbox offers.

After you learn the basics of how to select any sequence of tracks on your CD player, you may wish to take a look at the section entitled *Tips for Useful Programming of Your CD Player*.

Common Sense Precautions

Since each of these tools is a highly potentized sound, it is essential to exercise common-sense precautions. The effects of these sounds will

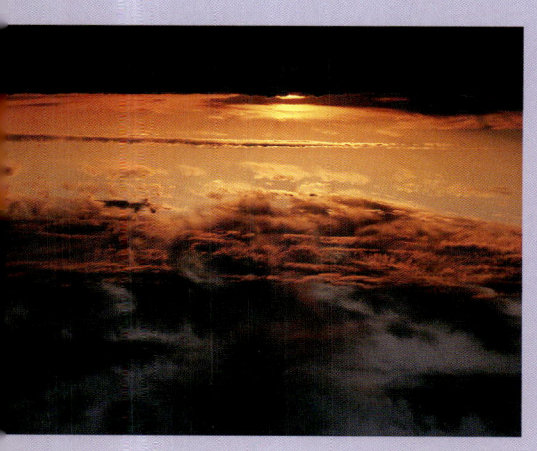

vary from individual to individual, and for each person the effects will vary from day to day—even hour to hour. If these sounds ever cause discomfort, immediately lower the volume or press *STOP*—whatever it takes to stop the discomfort. If you are part of a large group listening to these sounds, and one particular sound makes you uncomfortable, we suggest leaving the room right away. Any discomfort is a sign that it is not the right time for you to hear a particular sound. The normal effects of these sounds is to *increase* comfort and well-being.

The other common-sense precaution is not to listen to these sounds while driving or while controlling any potentially dangerous equipment.

Intuitive Guidance

The information contained herein was received inwardly—as were the sounds themselves—from a light being named Vista. Since the current level of our science can primarily measure effects only on the physical dimension, and since most of these effects occur on other dimensions, science can neither prove nor disprove this information. I leave it to your intuition and discernment to experience these sounds and this information with the innocence of a playful child, and then to use your discernment to determine for yourself what truth this holds for you.

IASOS

1. Pleiadian Healing Cycles   (3:28)

Optimum reception posture: Lying on your back.

This sound has two components: bells and gongs and the water sounds. The sudden beginning of the bells and gongs tends to "shake energy loose," after which the entire system tends to re-arrange itself into a more coherent pattern, due to the sustaining bell harmonics. Then the water sounds tend to wash away any energy that has shaken loose and does not really belong with you.

Accordingly, this sound has both a shake-up and a re-integration effect and also a cleansing effect. It tends to cause subtle body re-organization toward greater coherency and also a removal of accumulated energetic debris.

2. A Crystal Fountain Of Light (2:18)

Optimum reception posture: Spine-straight, sitting or standing. Headphones are highly recommended!

This sound is useful for stimulating and activating the crown chakra and the chakra directly above the crown chakra (a few inches above the head, directly above the spine).

It is also helpful for filling your subtle bodies with light. It is useful when applied with any visualization or intent to fill yourself with light.

If you ask your Higher Self to merge your future light body with your present self, this sound can potently activate this merger. Because it increases the resonance between your future light body self and your present self, it promotes light body activation. This also has a general stimulating and waking-up effect on any sluggish energy systems.

3. Cloud Prayer (5:06)

Optimum reception posture: Any position that promotes rest and centering for you.

This sound has a profound calming effect. It can be used for transforming emotional agitation or an overly excited state into a deep, restful calm. It can also transform a calm state into a state of profound stillness. The more still the waves are on a pond's surface, the more detail you can perceive through the waves to see what is on the bottom. Likewise, since water corresponds to the emotions, the more emotionally still you can become, the more easily and clearly you can receive inner guidance—from your Higher Self, your guides, your angels, or any Light Being.

Profound emotional stillness promotes transparency in inner reception. Hence the expression, "Be still and know that I am God." This music can help induce such profound stillness.

Finally, this music is effective at inducing a sense of sacredness, which can be useful in a wide variety of sacred activities.

An extended continuous half-hour version of *Cloud Prayer* is available on Iasos' *Timeless Sound* album.

4. Fairy Dust (2:43)

Optimum reception posture: Any position is fine.

This sound has a strong resonance at the highest frequencies a CD can reproduce. Consequently, effective application of this sound can only come from speakers or headphones that effectively reproduce very high frequencies.

Fairy Dust produces a highly stimulating effect on your etheric body. It enlivens and vitalizes your etheric body and sensitizes you to subtler energies.

Fairy Dust also produces a most interesting side effect: it tends to attract beings from the magical elemental nature kingdom: elves, gnomes, nature-spirits, and fairies. This is because this sound has a strong resonance with the actual real substance called "fairy dust."

All the beings in the elemental kingdom are specialists at transforming mental patterns into etheric patterns and then transforming etheric patterns into actual physical patterns—such as a flower or leaf. These beings can condense and solidify their own life essence on the etheric level into tiny golden liquid bubbles of living light—this is what "fairy dust" actually is! If you befriend the fairies in your own backyard, you can actually ask them to sprinkle you with their fairy dust, which will have an even more stimulating effect on your etheric body than this sound. At any rate, this sound makes them feel right at home—even in the midst of a man-made environment. If you want to attract these beings, just repeatedly play this sound (cycle-repeat) where they can hear it.

5. Woomfas (Interstellar Thunder) (1:44)

Optimum reception posture: Squatting.

Effective application of this sound* cannot come from tiny speakers. You need speakers or headphones that can really reproduce deep, bassy frequencies. These very bassy sounds have a potent resonant interaction with your base chakra—the energy center at the base of your spine. They have an even more powerful resonance with the chakra directly below your base chakra, the chakra a few inches below your spine.

This sound can be used for thawing out any base chakra that has become energetically frozen as the result of some past trauma. For those whose higher chakras are more activated than their base chakra, this sound can be used to vitalize and energize the base chakra and to create a better balance with the other chakras.

This sound can also be used for grounding. The grounding effect is more pronounced when the person simultaneously visualizes a beam of white light passing through the spine from above and anchoring solidly into the center of the earth.

Finally, this sound can energize your feminine connection to the earth by vitalizing and enlivening the chakra which is a few inches below your base chakra. The specialty of this chakra is to connect and ground you to the earth.

---

*The Woomfas used for this sound are a further development of the Woomfas at the beginning of *Blue Fire Realms* from the *Elixir* album by IASOS.

6. Glitter Sweep (Etheric Brush) (1:28)

Optimum reception posture: Lying on your back or standing.

Just as a brush sweeps through your hair, straightening it out and removing any kinks, this sound performs an analogous function etherically. This etheric brush smoothes out your energy flow channels and removes any kinks (local blockages in the energy channels) along the way. It thereby promotes a smooth unobstructed energy flow through your etheric energy channels. It is often a useful tool to play at the end of a session.

If this sound is heard with stereo headphones, it also tends to balance the left and right brain hemispheres.

7. The Transmuting Violet Flame Sound (4:58)

Optimum reception posture: Standing with arms out-stretched.

The transmuting violet flame is a higher-dimensional energy that is specifically designed to purify the substance or matter of various dimensions. For example, it can clear etheric blocks, melt away dense emotional energies, or cleanse karmic accumulations. This intelligent substance can respond to mental intent and the heart's desires. In fact, the Violet Flame Angels dedicate their entire service to bringing and dispensing this energy whenever and wherever it is called and requested.

When this flame-like energy is invoked (invited and requested), it descends down into the physical dimension as a violet ray, and then etherealizes back up as violet flames. In this process of dimensionally returning home, this energy functions as an inter-dimensional cleanser. It purifies all the substances it passes through—simply by raising their vibrations to significantly higher frequencies! Dense matter cannot stay around higher frequency matter and is centrifugally thrown off as the spin rates increase, like a wet dog throwing off water by quickly rotating along its spine.

Whenever you invoke the transmuting violet flame to pass through any aspect of your personal reality, the more vividly you can sense these energies, the more potently they can influence your energies.

The transmuting violet flame sound amplifies the vividness with which you sense these purifying flames, and thereby amplifies their effectiveness for you. And sensing these brilliant violet flames is really an exhilarating experience!

These sounds also provide the Violet Flame Angels with a familiar and comfortable acoustic environment within which to perform their service for you. Remember to thank these angels from your heart for their service to you. Your heart's gratitude, love, and appreciation is their tip for this service—and they love receiving it!

8. The Bubble Massage (4:26)

Optimum reception posture: Lying on your back.

Just as lying in a hot tub with the jacuzzi bubbles going can be very relaxing, the sound of bubbles can have a profoundly relaxing effect on all levels of your being, thereby decreasing the background noise in your energy systems. At the same time, these bubble sounds tend to produce a mild cleansing effect on your etheric body. If you listen with stereo headphones, you will also notice bubbles passing through your head.

9. Fairy Laughter (3:13)

Optimum reception posture: Any position is fine.

Laughter performs two wonderful functions on the emotional level. First, it brightens up your feelings, or perks you up. Technically, it raises the frequencies at which you are vibrating emotionally. You could think of laughter as "delight that is just boiling over."

Secondly, it dislodges and releases pockets of dense emotional energies within your field. Laughter is the emotional equivalent of soap suds. Just as soap loosens up dirt so it can get washed away more easily, laughter loosens up pockets of heavy emotions stuck in your emotional field (such as anger, annoyance, fear, sadness) so they can easily wash away into the light.

Because of emotional resonance, laughter is contagious. Just the *sound* of laughter can easily induce brighter feelings in others, and fairy laughter is one of the most potentized and high-frequency forms of laughter.

If your emotions effect your health, laughter truly is the best medicine!

10. Lagoon Waves (6:59)

Optimum reception posture: Lying on your back.

In many fields of understanding, water corresponds to the emotions and the emotional body. The sound of water in a very calm state has the effect of calming the emotions of the listener. Lagoon waves are the sound of water when it is very calm. If it were any calmer, the water would not even make a sound. Very little man-made music can calm the emotions as effectively as the sound of very calm waves.

Lagoon waves are often a useful tool to play at the end of a session. An effective combination of tools is alternating Fairy Laughter with Lagoon Waves, since they have complementary effects on the emotions: laughter enlivens and upshifts the emotions, while the waves calm them down and smooth them out.

11. Undulating Bell Harmonics (7:25)

Optimum reception posture: Lying on your back.

Imagine you are bathing in a liquid pool of bell harmonics that are slowly shifting. Each bell harmonic is a liquid version of a crystal tuning fork. As each harmonic continues slowly rippling through different frequencies, it occasionally passes through a frequency that is already alive and vibrating in one of your energy fields—one of your primary frequencies. When they are both vibrating at the same frequency, this bell harmonic resonates with your primary frequency, making it hum with more vitality.

These shifting bell harmonics also fine-tune the relationship between your other frequencies, so they become even more harmonically related with each other. In other words, they occasionally pass through a primary frequency of one of your energy fields and, when they do, they enliven this frequency and fine-tune it into a more coherent harmonic relationship with your other primary frequencies.

Also, any treatment or energetic work with crystals or crystal energies tends to be resonantly enhanced by these bell harmonics.

This sound is a brief excerpt from the 30-minute piece, *The Valley of Enchimed Peace*, from the *Jeweled Space* album by IASOS.

12. The Angels Of Purity (5:27)

Optimum reception posture: Any position is fine.

They say that harmony is the "keynote of heaven." Harmony refers to energy patterns that support and reinforce each other—as a living self-sustaining system, rather than interfering with each other and eventually canceling each other out. Coherence means a high level of harmony, or integration, within the energy patterns of any system. Harmony and coherence point in the direction of increased health, life, and well-being. Lack of harmony points in the direction of decay, disease, and discomfort.

Your various energy bodies (e.g., your physical body, etheric body, emotional body, and mental body) are all continuously influencing each other. Since a rather large portion of your life force passes through your emotional body, that body has an especially potent affect on your other bodies.

Harmonious music tends to induce harmonious emotions, which in turn influence your other bodies to resonate in harmony, thus inducing good health. Harmonious music can start a chain reaction of increased coherence/harmony that begins as sound, and ultimately increases coherence, order, and well-being in all your bodies. This is one of the primary ways that music healing works. It is not really the music that causes the healing, but your emotions. All the music does is influence your emotions.

   The Angels of Purity contains a highly concentrated amount of musical harmony that soaks your emotional body in a bath of extreme harmony. To the extent that your emotional body responds to this harmony, it influences your other bodies to likewise resonate into a highly refined state of harmony, order, and coherence. And all this happens with the effortless ease of simply listening.

This version of The Angels of Purity is an excerpt from the full piece with this same name that will be released in an new album by IASOS. Please inquire.

13. Brooks (6:14)

Optimum reception posture: Lying on your back.

  The sound of a vibrant brook with vital rushing water tends to induce energy flow. Consequently, this sound can be used any time and anywhere you wish to transform sluggish or stagnant energy into a healthy, vital flowing current of energy. It helps stuck energy get unstuck. This effect is further enhanced with the use of headphones, which creates the sense that you are not nearby but right inside the brook. You are amidst the bubbling water as it flows downstream.

14. The Spiral Ascensions (2:29)

Optimum reception posture: Spine *very* straight—standing or sitting. Headphones highly recommended!

Within your spinal cord is a pillar of light, or a tube of your life essence. It connects all your energy centers (chakras) and continues upward as an electronic channel toward the God/Goddess source of your own being. It is truly your "life line."

These three ascension waves are specifically designed to clear the energy flowing through your pillar of light and to remove any blocks along the way. Having your spine extremely straight facilitates this process. Each of these sounds begins at the lower energy centers and moves progressively upward along this tube, until it vanishes while traveling upward along your life line.

You can ride this sound upward along your "life-line" to the higher octaves of your own being. To do so, you must enter into this experience with this clear intention. In addition, many people find this sound useful as an enhancer for numerous ascension-related activities.

15. Silence (1:00)

Optimum reception posture: Whatever position you are already in is just fine.

This one minute of silence is not intended as a joke, but performs the useful function of creating a space or silence or pause between other tracks. Since this selection, track #15, is one minute of silence, you can insert a pause of any length that is a multiple of one minute. For example, for a three minute pause, you can program this track to play three times in a row.

Here are the three ways of how to use Silence:

To create a pause between other tracks, in a sequence of tracks.
For example, if you wish to have a sequence with track 9, and track 2, then three minutes of silence, and then track 4,

program = 9, 2, 15, 15, 15, 4.

To create a pause before each repeat of the entire sequence.
For example, if you have a sequence of tracks 5, 8, and 3, and you want two minutes of silence before this entire sequence repeats,
program = 5, 8, 3, 15, 15
repeat = on.

To create a delayed beginning for a track or a sequence of tracks.
For example, if you have a sequence of tracks 7, 1, and 3, but you do not want this to begin until four minutes after you press *play*,
> program = 15, 15, 15, 15, 7, 1, 3.

Tips for Programming Your CD Player

Here are a few examples of what you might like to achieve with programming your CD player and how to proceed to get what you want:

You want to play just 1 track only once, without playing anything else afterwards:
If selected track is #7:
        program = 7   *repeat* = off [1]

You want to play just 1 track a precise number of times and then stop:
If selected track is #7 and you want it to play just three times:
        program = 7, 7, 7   *repeat* = off

You want to play just one track, but keep repeating it, until you press stop:
If selected track is #7:
        program = 7   *repeat* = *on*

---

[1] *Repeat* means *Repeat* or *Loop* or *Cycle* the track-selection(s).

You want to play just one track, but keep repeating it, with a pause just before each repeat:
If selected track is #7 and you want a three minute pause[2] before each repeat:
        program = 7,15,15,15   *repeat = on*

You want to play a sequence of tracks only once and then stop:
If the selected tracks are #7, #2, and #9, program the following:
        program = 7,2,9   *repeat = off*

You want to play a sequence of tracks and keep repeating the entire sequence, until you press stop:
If the selected tracks are #7, #2, and #9:
        program = 7,2,9   *repeat = on*

You want to play a sequence of tracks and keep repeating the entire sequence, with a pause just before each repeat:
If the selected tracks are #7, #2, and #9, and you want a three minute pause:
        program = 7,2,9,15,15,15   *repeat = on*

---

[2] The *Silence* track, which is used as a pause, is #15, and it is precisely one minute of silence.

You want to play a sequence of tracks, but want to include a pause before you start the sequence:
If the selected tracks are #7, #2, and #9, and you want a three minute wait before the sound begins:

    program = 15,15,15,7,2,9   *repeat* = off

You want to play a sequence of tracks, but wait before you start the sequence. And keep repeating the sequence, but again wait before each repeat of the sequence:
If the selected tracks are #7, #2, and #9, and you want a three minute wait before the sound begins, and a 3 minute pause before each repeat of the sequence,

    program = 15,15,15,7,2,9   *repeat* = on

You want to play a sequence of tracks, but with a pause between the second and third selections:
If the selected tracks are #7, #2, and #9, and you want a three minute pause between the second and third selections:

    program = 7,2,15,15,15,9   *repeat* = off

You want to keep playing and repeating a sequence of tracks, but for each repeat have a pause between the second and third selections:
If the selected tracks are #7, #2, and #9, and you want a three minute pause between the second and third selections:

    program = 7,2,15,15,15,9   *repeat* = on

Sound as Healing Light Waves

Healing is not creating something new, but merely re-aligning the body with its own already-existing divine blue-print. Healing is re-establishing a dynamic state of balance out of a temporary state of imbalance. There are innumerable ways to do this; using sound is one potent way.

How is it that sound can heal?

Sound heals primarily through physical resonance and emotional resonance. *Resonance* means that two energy systems are capable of vibrating at the same frequency, and if one of them starts vibrating, and is sufficiently near the other, it will tend to cause the other to also vibrate at this frequency. For example, if you tune two strings on a guitar to the same note (frequency), and you pluck one of these strings, the other will also start vibrating.

Physical resonance results from the vibrating air shaking up the molecules and causing the energy system to synchronize with itself into standing waves. These waves produce order, symmetry, coherency, and stability out of random chaos. In his study of *cymatics,* Hans Jenny shows photographs of beautifully symmetric shapes that were formed by randomly arranged powder on a surface that was caused to vibrate by sound from an attached speaker.

Sound can produce order out of randomness by causing an energy system to synchronize with itself, producing standing waves. Standing waves are inherently self-reinforcing and accordingly tend to maintain their existence.

They are a fundamental characteristic of any self-organizing system, such as your body, and this increased coherency leads to increased health, longevity, and greater life force. Sound can cause the various parts of your body to synchronize with each other, such as your heart beat synchronizing with your breathing and with your brain waves. Any system that self-synchronizes into standing waves causes these waves to reinforce each other (sustained good health). In a vibrating system without standing waves, however the waves tend to randomly cancel each other out (leading to disease and death).

Shaking up the molecules for sound healing through physical resonance can occur, for example, by toning with your voice or using gongs or Tibetan bowls rubbed in a circular fashion. A more esoteric example is dolphins that use their sonar to tune-up the chakras of humans who are swimming with them. This type of sound healing (physical resonance) usually does not involve a complex blend of many instruments, such as an orchestra, but only one potent sound by itself.

Emotional resonance means that music influences your feelings, and your feelings directly affect your health. To properly understand this, you must understand how different dimensions can influence each other. Then you can apply this understanding to your physical, emotional, and mental bodies, each of which is vibrating in a different dimension, or a different range of frequencies.

Because of resonance, two systems tuned to the same frequency can have an *energy-transfer* between them. A simple example of resonance is a radio. When your radio dial is tuned to the same carrier frequency a partcular radio station is transmitting, this resonance allows your radio to pick up and hear the program from that radio station.

Resonance also applies to the law of octaves. An octave higher means precisely twice the frequency and an octave lower means precisely half that frequency. For example, if "A" on a piano is 440 cycles per second, then 880 cycles per second is the "A" one octave higher and 220 cycles per second is the "A" one octave lower.

Resonance can and does occur between octaves, simply because their frequencies are precise whole-number multiples of each other. For example, if two strings on a guitar are tuned to 440 and 880 cycles per second, plucking either string will cause the other to also vibrate, thanks to resonance with the law of octaves. Keeping this in mind, you can see how each of your bodies (physical, emotional, mental) can influence each other.

Now to state the obvious:
1. *Sound and music influence your emotions.* This is an energy transfer from the physical plane to the emotional plane. Furthermore,
2. *Your emotions influence your physical body.* This is an energy transfer from the emotional plane back to the physical plane. Therefore:
3. *Harmonious music/sound* ⇨ *harmonious feelings* ⇨ *good health.* Furthermore,
4. *Your emotions influence your thinking.* This is an energy transfer from the emotional plane to the mental plane. And,

5. *Your thinking influences your physical body.* This is an energy transfer from the mental plane to the physical plane. Specifically, your cells respond to the mental pictures you hold in your mind of how your body is supposed to behave. Your beliefs about how your body is supposed to be will have long-lasting effects in how your body actually does behave. Therefore:
6. *Harmonious music/sound* ⇨ *harmonious feelings* ⇨ *optimistic thoughts* ⇨ *good health.* So to summarize, sound healing through emotional resonance triggers a chain reaction between dimensions that begins as physical dimension sound and, through the law of octaves, passes through your emotional body and mental body, and then both your emotional and mental bodies influence the state of health of your physical body.

Please do not infer from this that you should repress or suppress inharmonious feelings. When you find yourself in such a state, the worst thing you can do is repress or suppress your feelings. The healthiest thing to do is to express them, release them, clear them, and be done with them. Study children—they're great at this! It is the long-term sustaining of inharmonious emotions that provides a supportive environment for poor health. The ideal, of course, would be to create your reality in such a way that inharmonious emotions seldom get triggered in the first place.

Here's what happens when you repress/suppress your feelings. Your emotions are an egg-shaped energy field larger than your physical body that surrounds and interpenetrates your physical body. Each emotion is usually localized in one part of this emotional energy field. For example, anger might be localized in your solar plexus. Often, a person decides that their emotion is bad, shameful, or too painful and consequently decides to *not* let themselves feel it. This causes the area where this emotion exists to freeze up or lock up. Since the flow of prana or life-force is extremely interactive with the flowing of emotional energy, if emotional energy freezes up in one area, the flow of life force also freezes up in that area. Whatever physical organs happen to occupy the space where the emotional energy got stuck will no longer receive sufficient life force. If this condition persists, those physical organs will begin having serious health problems.

The solution:

Let yourself feel the feelings!
Get the emotions flowing! *

All diseases are really psychosomatic (caused by the mind and feelings). The physical body is the realm of effect. The realm of cause is your thoughts and feelings. You can think of your physical body as the accumulated repository or record of all your thoughts and feelings throughout your life.

The Angels of Healing make an important distinction between a temporary healing and a permanent healing. For them, temporary healing occurs when only the symptoms (effect) are removed, not the cause. Permanent healing occurs when the emotional and mental attitudes creating the disease (cause) are changed or corrected. You can temporarily remove symp-

---

*emotion = energy in motion

toms, but for a permanent cure, you must remove the cause, and the cause is always in the thoughts and feelings.

Furthermore, new incoming thoughts have to pass through your intellectual censor, where you decide to accept or reject those ideas. However, music is sneaky. Sound and music by-pass any intellectual censor and totally saturate your emotions and feelings with their influence. This highlights the importance of taking dominion over your own world and always monitoring the music you allow into your emotional world.

For those of you who actively create sound and/or use sound in your work, remember that intent can modulate (ride on) a sound wave, just as one water wave can ride on top of another, larger wave. For example, the vowel sound of "ah" can make a plant shrivel up or thrive, depending on the intent of the singer in that moment. Maximize your intention when using sound. Clearly, consciously intend the effects of the sounds you are creating or using, and watch the impact blossom right before your eyes. Intention creates an effect not only when you are creating sounds, but even when you are re-playing sound recordings created by others.

One area of sound healing that is seldom regarded as such is rhythmic dance music. How so? Rhythmic dance music can perform three powerful healing functions:

1. It can charge the bottom three chakras —the base of the spine, the sex center, and the solar plexus center.
2. It can help ground the physical body.
3. It can vitalize the physical body by pumping energy into it.

Rhythm is actually an energy-pump through time. If it is an effective rhythm (the kind where you have to move), then it is pumping a lot of energy. Effective rhythms tend to induce a resonance between the pulsing sound waves and the pulsing body waves. When the resonance is great, there is a hi-tech name for this synchronized pulsing together of sound waves and body waves—dancing!

Since resonance allows for energy-transfer, in such a synchronized state, the sound of the music you are dancing to can actually pump energy and vitality into your body! ("I could have danced all night...") In this way, rhythm provides nourishment to your body.

The trick is to only choose dance music that is emotionally positive. Otherwise you can pollute your emotional body while vitalizing your physical body. Be discerning. Only choose dance music that you sense to be emotionally positive and uplifting. Trust your intuitive guidance on this.

Another area of sound healing is sacred music. Here's how this works. Whatever you place your attention on, your attention is like an electronic beam that instantly connects you to the target of your attention, like dialing a particular phone number. Think of this beam of your attention as a wire on the mental plane, connecting two points. While this electronic beam of your attention is connecting you to your attention-target, three things occur:

1. Your energy flows out to the object of your attention.
2. The energy from the object of your attention flows back to you.
3. By being electronically linked together, you and this object of your

attention begin to synchronize, and entrain, and resonate together as one system.

Whether your attention is focused on television reporting some horrible disaster or on a beautiful flower, you and the object of your attention immediately begin resonating together as one synchronized system. Immediately, you begin absorbing the qualities of that reality.

When your attention is on the one supreme source of all life everywhere, that which makes all of us alive, you begin resonating with this universal energy. This means you begin synchronizing with the entire universe. And since balance is one of the prime qualities of the universal source of all life, this means you are getting more in balance with the entire universe. And balance equals healing. Attuning to the universal source, by any means, is the most healing thing you can do for yourself.

However, most people have such a short attention span that even if their attention is on the one universal source, it cannot stay solidly focused there for more than a few seconds. This is where music can help. Music can perform the function of assisting you in attuning to the Universal first cause and in keeping your attention focused there for an extended period of time. Sacred music causes you to become healed by establishing a sustained alignment with the infinite eternal source of all life. For each second that your attention is focused on the universal source of all life, there is a tremendous stream of healing balancing energy flowing into your body and energy fields.

Readers who use sound professionally as a healing tool should keep in mind that there are endless, innumerable, countless ways that sound can be used for healing, and no one knows them all. Your mind is an automatic magnet for ideas in any field of reality that it specializes in. If your mind specializes in sound healing, your mind is a mental magnet for picking up ideas for unique new ways sound can be used for healing. So follow your hunches. Manifest those ideas—however far out they may seem. Implement those flashes. Enrich this planet with the sound-healing techniques and ideas you are receiving.

Having discussed sound as a healing modality, let me discuss some other uses of sound and music that are dear to my heart. I apologize in advance if this seems a bit too metaphysical for some of our readers.

Sound can be used as a channel-tuner for your consciousness. By tuning the antenna of your consciousness, you can more readily dial in and access specifically desired light realms. When sound helps you do this, the sound is functioning as a vibrational gateway to higher planes. Rather than the radio dial of your consciousness being stuck most of the time on only one station (this physical dimension), you can exercise your ability to access different realms (practice moving that dial). Once you familiarize yourself with these realms, you can readily access them without the music.

Furthermore, you can use sound as a wave guide to harmonically align with the higher octaves of your own being—your Higher Self. Through attention, you can dial in and travel through the various higher octaves, or floors, of your own God/Goddess Self. There are vast legions of beings, both in the angelic kingdom and in the elemental nature kingdom, whose specialty is the musical outpouring of divinity. In the angelic kingdom there are fleets of music angels ready and eager to instantly come where they are invoked and invited, to grace and join in with any ceremony, adding their uniquely exquisite energies to those of the humans.

Often humans do not hear the angels and do not even sense them, but they are nevertheless emotionally moved by them—to the very core of their souls. As our planet continues its dimensional up-shift, more and more ceremonies will consciously include and combine the angelic and elemental nature kingdoms with the human kingdom. Music can be the unifying force that resonates these three kingdoms together into a unified whole—for worship, adoration, and alignment with the one universal source that makes all of us alive.

These next few years, many musician light-workers will focus on creating music for all these purposes. Avail yourself of their sounds. Use sound to accelerate your evolution, rather than passively allowing sound to have a sluggish effect on your growth. Take charge of your life—choose the music you listen to. Look for music that is coherent, emotionally uplifting, and centering—music that comes from a loving heart. Ask your own heart: "How is this music affecting me, on all levels?" Trust what your heart tells you, and act on it. Choose and intend to effortlessly ride these sound waves gracefully upward toward your own expansions—on waves of light

Enthusiastically at your service,

Summary Of the Effects

1. Pleiadian Healing Cycles (3:28)
- * Shakes up and re-integrates: subtle body re-organization toward greater coherency and order
- * Cleanses: removes accumulated energetic debris

2. A Crystal Fountain Of Light (2:18)
- * Stimulates and activates the crown chakra
- * Fills your subtle bodies with light
- * Facilitates merging your future light body with your present self for light body activation
- * General stimulates and wakes up any sluggish energy systems

3. Cloud Prayer (5:06)
- * Profoundly calming
- * Induces profound stillness
- * Clear transparency in inner reception
- * Induces a sense of sacredness

4. Fairy Dust (2:43)
- * Highly stimulating on your etheric body
- * Sensitizes you to subtler energies
- * Attracts beings from the magical elemental nature kingdom: elves, gnomes, nature-spirits, and fairies

5. *Woomfas (Interstellar Thunder)* (1:44)
   * Thaws out any base chakra that has become energetically frozen from trauma
   * Vitalizes and energizes the base chakra
   * Grounding
   * Energizes your feminine connection to the earth

6. *Glitter Sweep (Etheric Brush)* (1:28)
   * Promotes smooth, unobstructed energy flow through your etheric energy channels by removing any local blockages
   * Balances the left and right brain hemispheres (when listening with headphones)

7. *The Transmuting Violet Flame Sound* (4:58)
   * Inter-dimensional cleansing
   * Amplifies the vividness with which you sense these purifying flames and thereby amplifies their effectiveness

8. *The Bubble Massage* (4:26)
   * Profoundly relaxing
   * Mild cleansing of your etheric body

9. *Fairy Laughter* (3:13)
   * Raises your emotional frequencies
   * Dislodges and releases accumulated pockets of low-frequency emotions

10. *Lagoon Waves* (6:59)
    * Calms the emotions

11. Undulating Bell Harmonics (7:25)
- Enlivens your primary frequencies
- Induces more coherent harmonic relationships between your primary frequencies
- Enhances working with crystals and crystal energies

12. The Angels Of Purity (5:27)
- Soaks your emotional body in a bath of extreme harmony

13. Brooks (6:14)
- Induces energy flow
- Helps stuck energy get unstuck
- Transforms sluggish or stagnant energy into a healthy vital flowing current of energy

14. The Spiral Ascensions (2:29)
- Clears the energy flowing through your pillar of light
- Removes any etheric blocks along your spine
- You can ride this sound upward along your life-line to the higher octaves of your own being
- Enhances any ascension-related activities

15. Silence (1:00)
- Allows you to schedule a pause between other tracks in a sequence of tracks

Table of Sound Tools

#	Tool	Time	Stimulating & Activating	Soothing & Relaxing	Cleansing & Purifying	Aligning & Increased Coherence
1	*Pleiadian Healing Cycles*	4:28			✿	✿
2	*A Crystal Fountain of Light*	4:58	✿		✿	
3	*Cloud Prayer*	5:06		✿		
4	*Fairy Dust*	2:43	✿		✿	
5	*Woomfas (Interstellar Thunder)*	1:44	✿			
6	*Glitter Sweep (Etheric Brush)*	1:28	✿			✿
7	*The Transmuting Violet Flame Sound*	4:58			✿	
8	*The Bubble Massage*	4:26		✿	✿	
9	*Fairy Laughter*	3:13	✿		✿	
10	*Lagoon Waves*	6:59		✿		
11	*Undulating Bell Harmonics*	7:25		✿		✿
12	*The Angels of Purity*	5:27			✿	✿
13	*Brooks*	6:14	✿			
14	*The Spiral Ascensions*	2:29	✿			✿
15	*Silence*	1:00		✿		

Also available from Iasos

Angelic Music
Extremely soothing and well suited to relax body and soul. It can be used for creating a sacred space, for meditating, body-work, emotional healing, tuning into angels and much more.

Timeless Sound
Two 30-minute pieces of smooth uninterrupted musical harmony.

Elixir
Iasos' most celestial album. Music filled with joyous sparkling light.

Bora Bora 2000
Angelic dance music. Invigorates and prevents the depleting effect so many dance albums have.

For a color brochure contact
Bluestar Communications
44 Bear Glenn
Woodside, CA. 94062
800-625-3378
web site: http://www.bluestar.com

To contact Iasos:
email: iasos@nbn.com
web site: http://iasos.com